Norma J. Cohen

Norma J. Cohen

WHO WOULD HAVE GUESSED?
IT'S ALL FOR THE BEST!

Written and illustrated
by Loren Hodes

Library of Congress Cataloging in Publication Data

Hodes, Loren.
   Who would have guessed? : it's all for the best! / written
and illustrated by Loren Hodes.
      p. cm.
   Summary: Upset at being left behind when all of his friends go to
summer camp, a young Jewish boy visits a clown who teaches him that
even seemingly bad things are ultimately for the best, and suggests
mitzvos he and a new friend can fulfill to spread the message to
others.
   ISBN-13: 978-1-932443-48-6 (hardcover)
   ISBN-10: 1-932443-48-7 (hardcover)
 [1. Commandments (Judaism)--Fiction. 2. Judaism--Customs and practices--
Fiction. 3. Jews--Fiction. 4. Clowns--Fiction. 5. Conduct of life--Fiction. 6.
Stories in rhyme.] I. Title. II. Title: It is all for the best!
   PZ8.3.H6653Wh 2006
   [E]--dc22
                              2006012323

THE JUDAICA PRESS, INC.
123 Ditmas Avenue / Brooklyn, NY 11218
718-972-6200 / 800-972-6201
info@judaicapress.com
www.judaicapress.com

Manufactured in China

For my beloved parents,
with eternal gratitude.
Loren

The Judaica Press, Inc.
www.judaicapress.com

FUN

GONE FISHING

SCHOOL

CLOSED

2

The first day of vacation dawned sunny and bright,
But the streets were all empty, no children in sight.
In cars, trains and buses, piled high with suitcases,
Off to camp they all went, with bright, happy faces.
Heading up to the mountains, for fresh air and sun,
For hikes in the woods, and weeks full of fun.

"Ima," begged Yaakov, "please let me go, too.
My friends are all gone. I'll have nothing to do."
"I'm sorry," sighed Ima, "we've decided not yet.
Another year older we'd like you to get."
Abba said, "Yaakov, summer has just begun.
Gam zu l'tova⋆—wait and see, you'll have fun."

⋆"This, too, is for good."

4

"It's not fair!" thought Yaakov.
   "It really can't be!
Why should the one
   left behind here be me?

Why can't I go to camp,
   like the rest?
I really don't see
   how it's all for the best."

He walked along sadly
and heaved a big sigh,
Then suddenly stopped.
Something strange caught his eye.

It shined and it gleamed
with a shimmering light.
A card with a clown—
what an interesting sight!

"Wow, it's amazing," a shocked
Yaakov said.
He picked it up, opened it, and
here's what he read:

Gumzy L. Tova

If things aren't right or going
    your way,
It's time to do something
    to brighten your day.
There's really no reason
    to feel sad at all,
A qualified Clown is the
    one you should call.

My specialty is seeing good
    everywhere.
My business is *simcha**
    and making it clear!
To trust that Hashem knows
    what is best for you,
Call Gumzy L. Tova—
    and I will help you!

Gumzee me!

* happiness

9

"I really should call him," Yaakov thought with a sigh
"I'm upset about camp. It's sure worth a try.
I'll ask Ima," he said, as he quickly ran home.
"She taught me to never meet strangers alone."

"Gumzy L. Tova?" Ima said. "Rings a bell…
Why yes, now I know. I remember him well!
I was much younger then, maybe your age,
When my friends and I went to go see him on stage."

11

"You see, we were bored,
and had nowhere to go,
But he soon had us laughing
with his sidesplitting show.

Gumzy taught us a lesson
that has stood to the test,
About trusting that everything
is for the best."

"You've reached the voice message
of Gumzy the Clown
For me there's no reason to ever get down.
So pay me a visit, please come and say 'Hi.'
I'll teach you my tricks. Just come right on by.
To find me at once, keep a smile
on your face.
Just follow your nose and you'll soon
find my place."

aid Ima, "I think he's someone
you should meet,
's not every day that you'll have
such a treat.
ome on and I'll drive you,
I'd love to say 'Hi,'
nd thank him for
teaching me how
a Jew should
get by!"

Soon Yaakov and Ima
were standing before
Gumzy L. Tova's
bright yellow door.

13

Before they could knock, the door opened wide,
A clown bellowed, "Greetings! Do please step inside."
There stood Gumzy, dressed neat as a pin,
With a polka-dot tie and a twinkly grin.

"Hi! I'm Gumzy L. Tova!
    Gumzoglad you've come!
What is your name? Where
    are you from?

Would you like a cold
    drink? Would you like
    to see tricks?
If you like, I can juggle
    with eight or nine sticks.

I can walk on my nose,
    I can walk on my head,
Or do a hundred
    and twenty-six
    cartwheels instead.

A qualified Clown,
    I always say,
Should always be able to
    brighten your day."

Yaakov was glad he'd found a new friend.
He told Gumzy his problem
    from beginning to end.
"My friends went to camp,
    and I couldn't go.
My Ima and Abba still want me to grow.
I wanted to go, just like all the rest,
But Abba told me that it's all for the best."

"Abba is right,"
    Gumzy said with a smile.
"You'll see for yourself,
    but it may take a while.
Sometimes life's a challenge;
    sometimes it's a test,
But a Jew must believe
    that it's all for the best.

"You must trust that Hashem
 knows the best way for you.
It's *emunah**, *bitachon***
 that help us get through.
Now listen with care
 to the words that I say.
I think they will help you
 to see things my way.

When kids go away, it's fun for them, true,
But back home there is so much
 for others to do.
There are so many *mitzvos**** you can fulfill.
You could help someone out. It would give
 you a thrill.
My Still-To-Do list I'm sure holds the key.
The choices are many; let's look and see.

*faith; **trust in G-d; ***good deeds

"There's old Mrs. Kaye,
   all alone with her cat.
She'd love someone to visit
   for tea and a chat.

Mr. Gold is at home with
   a cold in the head.
He's got shopping to do,
   but he can't leave his bed.

18

"And sweet Mrs. Sax,
with children galore,
Needs a sitter to watch them,
just to go to the store.

"But here's a suggestion.
    I think this will do.
You could help someone out
    and make a friend, too.
This someone is Eli.
    He's not feeling great.
He's sad and he's lonely…
    I think you'll relate.

He's lying in bed with his leg in a cast.
He needs cheering up and it needs to be fast.
His friends are not home, so there's no one to say,
'Keep your chin up and smile! I'll be over to play!'
It would really be great, if you could, if you would,
Remind him that everything is for the good."

It didn't take long till Yaakov stood by the bed
Where Eli lay sadly, as Gumzy had said.
Yaakov came laden with books and with tapes,
With games and with goodies in all kinds of shapes.
"Come on," Yaakov said, "this is no way to be.
No need to feel lonely, 'cause now you have me!"

Soon both boys were busy and having such fun,
A beautiful friendship had clearly begun.
They played every game and they read every book.
They laughed till they ached and Eli's bed shook.

Then Gumzy arrived with balloons and a trick.
"It's a *mitzvah*," he said, "to go visit the sick.

"Well, I can see you're both having a ball!
You're happy and smiling and standing up tall.
And to think that this morning you both felt upset,
But things seem so different now since you boys met.
Things don't always happen as we think they should,
But a Jew must remember, it's all for the good!"

23

When Eli got well, the boys kept on doing
The marvelous tasks that Gumzy kept brewing!
They checked off each item on Gumzy's long list,
And made sure no *mitzvah* was left out or missed.

Mrs. Kaye and her cat
were so happy to chat.

They did Mr. Gold's
shopping in two
minutes flat,

Watched six little children
    and helped Mrs. Sax,
Played with them,
    read to them,
    fed them
    good snacks.

Their days were so busy with so much to do,
Vacation soon ended. The time simply flew!
"Abba was right," Yaakov thought, "after all.
The summer's been great! I'm having a ball!"

One day Gumzy said, "I'm in a gumzfix!
I need two boys like you to help out with my tricks.
The time has arrived, and I soon must be going,
But I know you two boys will keep the show showing."

So he taught them his secrets, the tricks of his trade,
And Gumzy was proud of the progress they made.
They learned how to walk on a string, upside down,
To joke and to juggle like any good clown.
They learned that a smile is the very best way
To brighten the dullest and dreariest day.

Soon Gumzy said,
  "I can see you two know
How to put on
  the Yaakov and Eli Show!"

Now Yaakov and Eli go all over town
Teaching *gam zu l'tova*—how not to get down.
"If it wasn't for Gumzy, we'd never have met!
The lessons he taught us, we'll never forget.
So the next time you're worried that something's
    not right,
Sing '*Gam zu l'tova!*' with all of your might.
You might think at the time that
    it's not a fair test,
But remember, only Hashem
    truly knows what is best!"

Eliyahu HaNavi said to Rav Beroka, "Those two people have a share in the world to come." Rav Beroka approached them and asked, "What is your job?" They said to him, "We are entertainers. We cheer up those who are sad."

(Talmud *Ta'anis* 22a)

No matter what happened to Nachum Ish Gamzu, he would always say, "*Gam zu l'tova*—this, too, is for the best."

(Talmud *Ta'anis* 21a)

It was taught in the name of Rabbi Akiva: A person should always say, "Whatever Hashem does is for a good purpose."

(Talmud *Brachos* 60b)